# THE TALKING MICKEY MOUSE SHOW™

# The Missing Meatball

**W•W**
**WORLDS OF WONDER®**

© MCMLXXXVII The Walt Disney Company. ℗ MCMLXXXVII Buena Vista Distribution Co., Inc. All rights reserved. Worlds of Wonder, Inc. is the exclusive licensee, manufacturer and distributor of The Talking Mickey Mouse Show toys. Mickey Mouse and Mickey Mouse characters are trademarks of The Walt Disney Company, Burbank, California. The symbol W•W is a trademark and "WORLDS OF WONDER" is a registered trademark of Worlds of Wonder, Inc., Fremont, California 94538.

Printed in U.S.A./P35                    ISBN: 1-55578-308-2

**Mickey**   I was standing on a ladder by my front door replacing a light bulb, when Goofy burst in.

**Goofy**   Hey, Mickey, wait'll you hear this!

**Mickey**   Watch out for the ladder, you'll—whoa, look out!

**Goofy**   I've got you, Mick.

**Mickey**   Nice catch, Goofy.

**Goofy**   Gee, thanks. You know, you should be more careful. You could have had a nasty fall if I hadn't been here.

**Mickey**    I'll, uh, try to watch it, Goofy. But you sounded like you had some big news. What's up?

**Goofy**    I just got a letter from my cousin Tony Goofioli, in Italy. Listen to this: "Cousin Goofy, you must come to Rome! I have just been made chef at a wonderful new restaurant. Please, you and your friend Mickey come to our grand opening."

**Mickey**    Gosh, I've always wanted to see Rome.

**Goofy**    Well, what are we waiting for? Let's hit the road.

**Mickey**    That's fine, Goofy. Just don't hit the ladder.

| **Goofy** | When our plane landed in Rome, my cousin Tony was there to meet us. |
| **Tony** | Goofy! Mickey! I am so glad to see you. Come, we will go straight to the restaurant. You must meet Sophia, my boss. She has a wonderful idea for the grand opening. |
| **Goofy** | That sounds great, Tony. |
| **Mickey** | Let's go! |

**Mickey**   When we got to the restaurant, Sophia came out to meet us.

**Goofy**   Yeah, and she gave us all a big kiss on the cheek!

**Sophia**   Welcome to Sophia's! Tony has told me so much about you.

**Goofy**   Thank you, ma'am. We're sure excited about your grand opening.

**Mickey**   Tony says you've put him in charge of something special.

**Sophia**   Oh, yes! To get publicity for my new restaurant, I asked Tony to cook the world's biggest meatball. Tomorrow all the press is invited and Tony will unveil his creation.

| | |
|---|---|
| **Goofy** | Hey, that's pretty good! And you've got a great location, too. You're right next door to the famous Leaning Tower of Pizza. |
| **Mickey** | No, Goofy, you're thinking of the Leaning Tower of Pisa. This building next to Sophia's is just a restaurant. |
| **Tony** | It is owned by Sophia's ex-partner, Dino Merlino. |
| **Sophia** | He only wants to serve pizza! Tomorrow he will see what real Italian cooking should be! |

**Mickey**  The next morning, crowds of reporters showed up at Sophia's for the big event.

**Goofy**  Sophia went up onto a little stage Tony had built for the big meatball unveiling.

**Sophia**  Welcome, everyone! Behind this curtain is a piece of Italian cooking history—the first of many that will be coming to you from Sophia's Kitchen.

**Goofy**  Gawrsh, Mick, we're seein' history.

**Sophia**  Now my brilliant chef, Tony Goofioli, will unveil his creation—the world's biggest meatball!

**Mickey**   Goofy, wasn't that Tony's cue to open the curtain?

**Goofy**   It sure was. But nothing happened.

**Sophia**   Ladies and gentlemen, excuse us a moment while my friends and I check backstage.

**Mickey**   We went inside, but Tony wasn't there. Because everyone was waiting, Sophia pulled the curtain up herself, and the crowd let out a gasp.

**Goofy**    Mick! The meatball! It's gone!

**Sophia**    Oh, no! My beautiful meatball! She is missing!

**Mickey**    Look, there's a trail of spices and vegetables heading around the back of the restaurant. Follow me!

**Goofy**    Gawrsh, there's garlic, tomatoes, onions, and all kinds of stuff. That must be one spicy meatball.

**Mickey**  The trail of Tony's ingredients led down an alley to the street behind Sophia's Kitchen.

**Goofy**  Look, there goes a delivery truck. It's from that Leaning Tower of Pizza restaurant.

**Mickey**  And Dino is driving!

**Goofy**  Gawrsh, he's in an awful hurry.

**Mickey** Goofy, look over here by the curb.
**Goofy** It's Tony's chef hat!
**Sophia** That no good Dino! He kidnapped my chef and my meatball, too! He's trying to ruin me!
**Mickey** Let's go, Sophia. If we hurry, maybe we can catch up to him.

**Mickey**  We jumped into Sophia's car and took off through the streets of Rome, hot on Dino's trail.

**Goofy**  But when we stopped at a red light, the truck skidded around a corner and disappeared.

**Mickey**  I'm afraid we've lost his trail.

**Goofy**  Look, Mick, there's an outdoor wedding—and everybody's eating pizza!

**Mickey**  Excuse us, ma'am. Did you see a truck go by from the Leaning Tower of Pizza?

| | |
|---|---|
| **Bride** | Yes, and it delivered all this food. |
| **Sophia** | That lousy Dino put meatball toppings on every pizza! |
| **Mickey** | Which way did the truck go, ma'am? |
| **Bride** | Down that street. He just left a minute ago. |
| **Goofy** | We jumped back in the car and took off. |
| **Mickey** | Hang on, Goofy. I've always heard that driving in Rome is an adventure, but this is ridiculous! |

| **Goofy** | Hey Mick, look over there. Isn't that one of those historical Roman ruins? |
| **Mickey** | Yes, that's the Colosseum—and there's the pizza truck right in front of it! Let's park the car and get out. We may still have a chance to rescue Tony and the meatball. |
| **Goofy** | I hope so, Mickey. |

| | |
|---|---|
| **Mickey** | We sneaked up to the back of the pizza truck. |
| **Goofy** | Mick, this truck looks different somehow. |
| **Mickey** | Shh, quiet, Goofy. On the count of three, we'll open the doors and grab Tony and the meatball. Ready? One...two...three! |
| **Goofy** | It's movie people! |
| **Nicky** | Cut! What are you people doing?! Are you crazy?! |
| **Mickey** | Gosh, we're sorry, sir. We're looking for the world's biggest meatball. |
| **Nicky** | I am no meatball! I am Nicky Nickolini, the famous director of the art film. You have just interrupted the filming of my next epic, "Colosseum Cannelloni." |

**Goofy**   Mick, we've got the wrong truck. But wait! There goes Dino now.

**Nicky**   Not the famous Dino Martino! Where? Where is he?

**Mickey**   Sorry, Mr. Nickolini, but we're chasing someone named Dino Merlino.

**Nicky**   Then please, go away. I must finish my movie.

**Sophia**   Quick, boys, back to the car.

**Mickey**  Off we raced. Sophia weaved her way through traffic, and in no time we were closing the gap between us and Dino's delivery truck.

**Goofy**  Gawrsh, Mick, look up ahead. Haven't we seen that building somewhere before?

**Mickey**  You're right, Goofy. We've come all the way back to Sophia's Kitchen! I wonder what Dino's up to. Sophia, try to pull up next to him.

**Sophia**  All right, Dino, what did you do with my meatball?

**Dino**  You crazy! I no touch your silly meatball. I've been delivering my pizzas.

**Mickey**  If you didn't take the meatball, why did you pull away so fast when we saw you in the alley?

**Goofy**  Yeah, and why'd you keep running away from us when we were chasing you around town?

**Dino**  What are you talking about? I didn't even see you. I always drive fast so my pizzas stay nice and hot.

**Mickey**  And I suppose you just happened to put meatball topping on all those pizzas?

**Goofy**   Before Dino could answer, we heard somebody yelling in the distance.

**Tony**    Look out! Runaway meatball!

**Mickey**  It's Tony! He's chasing that meatball of his down the hill!

**Goofy**   And it's headed straight for us! Everybody, move out of the way!

**Mickey**  We dove for cover just as the meatball smashed Sophia's stage to bits.

| | |
|---|---|
| **Goofy** | Gawrsh, there are pieces of meatball everywhere . . . and they're pretty tasty, too. |
| **Mickey** | Look, here comes Tony. |
| **Tony** | My beautiful meatball! She is ruined! |
| **Mickey** | How did you get away from the kidnappers, Tony? |
| **Tony** | What kidnappers? |
| **Goofy** | The ones who took you and the meatball. |
| **Tony** | What are you talking about? *I* took the meatball. |

**Mickey**   You? But why?

**Tony**   I was so proud, I wanted to show it to my mama. She lives just up the hill.

**Goofy**   Gawrsh, you pushed it all the way up there?

**Tony**   Yes, and Mama was so happy she took these pictures of me and the meatball. See? I'm the one on the right.

**Mickey**   But Tony, what about the grand opening? Did you forget about it?

**Tony**   Just for a little while. Then I pushed the meatball back down the hill.

**Goofy**   I guess it came down faster than it went up, huh, Tony?

**Tony**   You can say that again.

**Sophia**   I'll tell you what *I* can say. You have ruined my restaurant before it even opened! Tony, you're fired!

**Mickey**    For the rest of the day we just sat around Tony's house. We talked to him and tried to make him feel better, but it was no use.

**Goofy**    Dinnertime came, but Tony couldn't stand the thought of Italian food. So we sent out for Chinese.

**Mickey**    When Goofy went to the door to get it, he noticed the evening newspaper on the front porch.

**Goofy**    Well, what do you know. Here's a picture of another giant meatball right here on the front page. Small world, isn't it?

**Mickey**    Tony got up and went over to look at the newspaper.

**Tony**    That's not another meatball. That's *my* meatball! Look at it crash into that stage!

**Mickey**    One of the photographers must have still been there when the accident happened.

**Goofy**    And look at the headline: "Runaway Meatball." Gawrsh, Tony, you're famous.

**Tony**    Yes, my friend. And now one thing is sure: Tony Goofioli will never work in this town again.

| | |
|---|---|
| **Mickey** | Just then the phone rang. |
| **Tony** | Hello? Yes, I saw the papers. I'm so sorry... |
| **Goofy** | Then all of a sudden, Tony's face brightened up and he smiled. |
| **Tony** | They are? You do? I can? Thank you so very much! |
| **Mickey** | Tony, who was it? What did they say? |
| **Tony** | That was Sophia. Because of the picture in the paper, her restaurant is crowded with people, and they all want meatballs! She wants me to come back and be her chef! |
| **Goofy** | That's great, Tony. I wasn't in the mood for Chinese food tonight anyway. |

**Mickey**   Later that evening, Goofy and I ate meatballs at Sophia's place, served by the chef himself.

**Tony**   Well, what did you think? Are they good?

**Mickey**   They sure are.

**Goofy**   I like them, too, Tony. I just have one complaint.

**Tony**   But I want my meatballs to be perfect. What's wrong?

**Goofy**   Next time, could you make them just a little bit smaller?